KALINZU

A STORY FROM AFRICA

Jeremy Grimsdell

Kingfisher Books

In the hot, bush-filled grasslands of East Africa lived a small buffalo calf called Kalinzu and her mother, Amani. They belonged to a large buffalo herd. Kalinzu was just one month old, so she always stayed close by her mother's side.

During the drowsy heat of the day, when the grasslands baked and the air shimmered, the buffaloes rested and wallowed. Kalinzu loved to watch the large bulls sinking gently into the cool, muddy pools.

But Kalinzu did not like the red-billed oxpeckers which often visited the herd. They rode on her back and tickled her nose and ears as they searched for ticks to eat.

She did everything she could to chase them away. She scratched...

and shook her head...

and kicked out to shake off the oxpeckers. But the annoying birds just came back again.

One moonlit night when the herd was grazing, Kalinzu and Amani heard a strange scuffling sound.
A sticky-tongued aardvark was attacking a termite mound with its powerful claws.

Scratch, snuffle, scratch. Kalinzu stopped to watch. After a while Amani nudged Kalinzu and walked ahead to join the herd.

Suddenly, out of the darkness, sprang three spotted hyenas. Flashing their terrible teeth, they formed a circle around Kalinzu and Amani.

Amani kept in front of Kalinzu, protecting her. She snorted and swung her sharp horns. But the attackers were fierce and quick. Terrified, Kalinzu bellowed out as they tried to cut her off from Amani.

The moment the buffaloes heard Kalinzu's cries they swung around. In a charge of dust and pounding hooves, they thundered towards the attackers.
The hyenas growled in alarm, turned tail and fled.

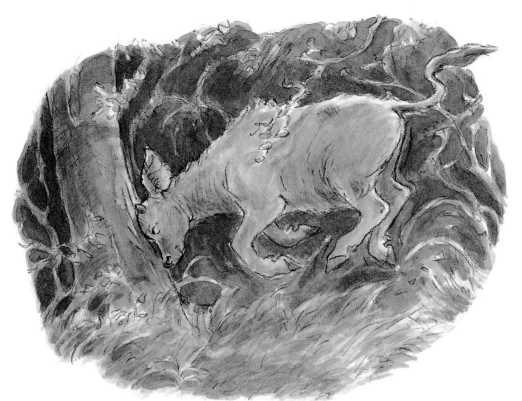

But in all the confusion, Kalinzu lost sight of Amani. She panicked and tore through a thick patch of bush. Then…CRASH!

Kalinzu lay very still on the ground. Her eyes were closed. She made no sound.

In the silvery moonlight, Amani searched and called for Kalinzu. She stopped, listening for an answering call, but none came. Later that night she returned to the herd, stopping to call and listen on her way.

When Kalinzu opened her eyes the sun was rising.
She got unsteadily to her feet. Where was her mother?
Where was the herd?

Trembling, she ran off through
the bush. She called for her
mother, but there was no reply.
As she searched she found…

a tall giraffe,

a family of warthogs,

and a large rhinoceros.
But the herd was
nowhere to be seen.

Kalinzu lifted her nose to the breeze, but still could not smell the herd. Again she called. Just then, two red-billed oxpeckers landed on her back. This time she did not try to shake them off.

The oxpeckers paused, looked around and flew off.
Kalinzu watched them as they flitted over some
thorn bushes.

Then, as they darted through a clump of Euphorbia
trees, she caught sight of the buffaloes.

There, at the edge of the herd, was Amani. Kalinzu began to call loudly and galloped towards her. Amani pricked up her ears and bellowed with joy.

Later that morning, as the day grew hotter, the herd moved off towards the cool, muddy wallows.

Kalinzu, with an oxpecker perched high on her back, stayed very close to Amani's side.